Dear Parents and Educators,

Welcome to Penguin Young Readers! As parents and educators, you know that each child develops at his or her own pace—in terms of speech, critical thinking, and, of course, reading. Penguin Young Readers recognizes this fact. As a result, each Penguin Young Readers book is assigned a traditional easy-to-read level (1–4) as well as a Guided Reading Level (A–P). Both of these systems will help you choose the right book for your child. Please refer to the back of each book for specific leveling information. Penguin Young Readers features esteemed authors and illustrators, stories about favorite characters, fascinating nonfiction, and more!

Meet Trouble

LEVEL 2

GUIDED READING LEVEL **E**

This book is perfect for a **Progressing Reader** who:
- can figure out unknown words by using picture and context clues;
- can recognize beginning, middle, and ending sounds;
- can make and confirm predictions about what will happen in the text; and
- can distinguish between fiction and nonfiction.

Here are some **activities** you can do during and after reading this book:
- Character Traits: Trouble is a funny kitten. Come up with a list of words that describe him.
- Discuss: Discuss the meaning of the word *trouble*. Why do you think the cat is named Trouble? If you had to think of another name for him, what would it be and why?

Remember, sharing the love of reading with a child is the best gift you can give!

—Bonnie Bader, EdM
  Penguin Young Readers program

*Penguin Young Readers are leveled by independent reviewers applying the standards developed by Irene Fountas and Gay Su Pinnell in *Matching Books to Readers: Using Leveled Books in Guided Reading*, Heinemann, 1999.

For Emily & Daisy—SH

Penguin Young Readers
Published by the Penguin Group
Penguin Group (USA) Inc., 375 Hudson Street, New York, New York 10014, USA
Penguin Group (Canada), 90 Eglinton Avenue East, Suite 700, Toronto, Ontario M4P 2Y3, Canada
(a division of Pearson Penguin Canada Inc.)
Penguin Books Ltd, 80 Strand, London WC2R 0RL, England
Penguin Ireland, 25 St Stephen's Green, Dublin 2, Ireland (a division of Penguin Books Ltd)
Penguin Group (Australia), 707 Collins Street, Melbourne, Victoria 3008, Australia
(a division of Pearson Australia Group Pty Ltd)
Penguin Books India Pvt Ltd, 11 Community Centre, Panchsheel Park, New Delhi—110 017, India
Penguin Group (NZ), 67 Apollo Drive, Rosedale, Auckland 0632, New Zealand
(a division of Pearson New Zealand Ltd)
Penguin Books (South Africa), Rosebank Office Park, 181 Jan Smuts Avenue,
Parktown North 2193, South Africa
Penguin China, B7 Jiaming Center, 27 East Third Ring Road North,
Chaoyang District, Beijing 100020, China

Penguin Books Ltd, Registered Offices: 80 Strand, London WC2R 0RL, England

Text copyright © 2001 by Susan Hood. Illustrations copyright © 2001 by Kristina Stephenson.
All rights reserved. First published in 2001 by Grosset & Dunlap, an imprint of Penguin Group (USA) Inc.
Published in 2013 by Penguin Young Readers, an imprint of Penguin Group (USA) Inc.,
345 Hudson Street, New York, New York 10014. Manufactured in China.

Library of Congress Control Number: 00107518

ISBN 978-0-448-42455-2   10 9 8 7 6 5 4 3 2 1

ALWAYS LEARNING   PEARSON

Meet Trouble

WITHDRAWN

by Susan Hood
illustrated by Kristina Stephenson

Penguin Young Readers
An Imprint of Penguin Group (USA) Inc.

Hello, Trouble!

This is Trouble.

Emily loves Trouble.

Trouble wants to be a good kitten.

Trouble tries to be a good kitten.

But Trouble gets into trouble.

Trouble gets into lots of trouble!

He just can't help it.

Pots clatter.

Papers scatter.

Plates shatter.

Paints splatter.

But Emily loves Trouble.

She just can't help it!

Double Trouble

Trouble wants to play.

He plays with his string.

He plays with his mouse.

What is that?

19

Trouble jumps up.

Look! It is a kitten!

Trouble hides.

The other kitten hides.

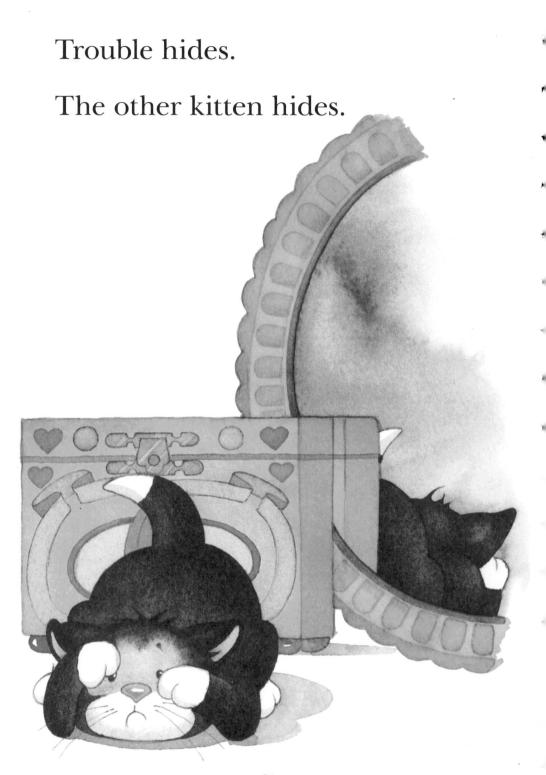

Trouble peeks out.

The other kitten peeks out.

Trouble waves his tail.

The other kitten waves his tail.

Trouble leaps!

The other kitten leaps!

BANG!

Silly Trouble!